Pip and Posy

www.worldofpipandposy.com

For Helen, and a big
thank you to Adélie
for her help
A.S.

First published 2013 by Nosy Crow Ltd
The Crow's Nest, 10a Lant Street
London SE1 1QR
www.nosycrow.com

This edition first published in 2015

ISBN 978 0 85763 383 5

Nosy Crow and associated logos are trademarks and/or registered
trademarks of Nosy Crow Ltd
Text © Nosy Crow 2013
Illustrations © Axel Scheffler 2013

The right of Axel Scheffler to be identified as the illustrator
of this work has been asserted.

A CIP catalogue record for this book is available from the British Library.

Printed in China by Imago

1 3 5 7 9 8 6 4 2

Pip and Posy
The Bedtime Frog

Axel Scheffler

nosy crow

Posy was going to
stay at Pip's house.

She packed up her suitcase very carefully.
She didn't want to forget anything.

Then she got on the bus.
She was very excited.

Pip was really happy
to see Posy.
"Hi, Posy!" he called.

"Hello, Pip!" giggled Posy.

Pip and Posy had lots of fun.
They played with Pip's cars.

They played with the farm.

And then they played a game called 'pirates in hospital'.

They ate
spaghetti.

They had a
bubbly bath.

They brushed
their teeth.

And they read
a funny story.
After that, it was
time for bed.

"Night-night, Posy," said Pip,
as he cuddled up with his piggy.

"Sweet dreams, Pip," said Posy.

They switched off their lights.

Pip was very nearly asleep
when he heard a voice.
"Froggy!" said the voice.

It was Posy.
"I've forgotten Froggy," she sniffed.

"I CAN'T SLEEP WITHOUT MY FROGGY!!"

Pip turned his light back on again.
"Would you like this teddy, Posy?" he said.

But Posy did not want Pip's teddy.
"It's not green," she said.
"My frog is green."

"Would you like my dinosaur?" said Pip.
"He's green."

"No!" said Posy.
"That dinosaur
is too big and too scary!"

"What about my frog
money box?" said Pip.

"No!" said Posy,
"That is the WRONG FROG!"

Posy cried and cried and cried.

Oh dear! Poor Posy.

Pip thought for a moment.
Then he did a **very difficult** thing.

"Would you like Piggy, Posy?" he said.

Posy stopped crying.
Piggy was an extremely nice pig.

"Yes, please, Pip," she said.

Soon Pip was asleep.

And so was Posy.

And the next day, when Posy
went home to her house,
she found her frog . . .

. . . exactly where
she had left him!

Hooray!